Aaron couldn't believe he had missed. He stood on the court with his hands on his hips, still staring at the basket. And that's when Jared charged toward him. "What were you thinking?" he yelled. "I was wide open under the basket. All you had to do was hit me."

Aaron turned away from Jared and started to walk toward the locker room.

"You think you can do it all alone," Jared was yelling at him. "You're good. But you're not half as good as you think you are."

Aaron knew what he wanted to say: "Half as good as I think I am is still twice as good as you." But he didn't say that or anything else. He just walked off the floor.

ONE-MAN TEAM

BY
DEAN HUGHES

Bullseye Books • Random House
New York

For Chad Garbe and Spencer Graves

A BULLSEYE BOOK PUBLISHED BY RANDOM HOUSE, INC.
Text copyright © 1994 by Dean Hughes
Cover illustration copyright © 1994 by Dennis Lyall

Library of Congress Cataloging-in-Publication Data
Hughes, Dean, 1943–
One-Man Team / by Dean Hughes
p. cm.
Summary: Although he is a basketball whiz, eighth-grader Aaron Reeves must
learn to be a team player in order to make friends on the basketball team at
his new school.
ISBN 0-679-85441-X (pbk.)
[1. Basketball—Fiction. 2. Interpersonal relations—Fiction.
3. Schools—Fiction.] I. Title.
PZ7.H873120p 1994 [Fic]—dc20 93-44676
RL: 5.4
First Bullseye Books edition: November 1994
Manufactured in the United States of America 10 9 8 7 6 5 4 3 2 1

chapter one

Aaron Reeves felt strange as he walked onto the court. The other players kept glancing toward him, seeming to size him up, but Aaron avoided any eye contact.

The guys were shooting around, waiting for the coach to get practice started. Aaron stepped inside the circle of boys and grabbed a rebound.

Someone said "hi" to Aaron. He nodded in the direction of the voice. Then he dribbled to the top of the key.

He rolled the ball in his hands and bounced it a couple of times. Then he turned and took a jump shot. Nothing fancy—just a straight-away jumper—but it popped the net, and now he could see that all the guys were watching him.

He grabbed another rebound, dribbled toward the corner, and put up a turn-around jumper that hit the bottom of the net. Then he slashed to the hoop, took the ball as it bounced off the floor, spun, and flipped a reverse lay-up off the glass—and in.

"Nice shot," somebody said.

Aaron said, "Thanks," but he didn't look at anyone.

Aaron had moved into town—Greenwood, Oregon—only a week before. He had registered for eighth grade at the middle school the next morning. But it was already January, and he had known that the basketball team was set for the season. So at the time, he had decided not to say anything to the coach. He figured he would just play some ball in gym class.

Aaron moved a lot—usually once or twice a year. His father supervised building for a big construction company, and his family moved each time a new project started. The company was putting up a shopping mall in this town. Aaron hoped it would be finished by August or so, and next year he could arrive somewhere just as school was starting—for once.

As it turned out, however, even though the timing had been wrong here in Greenwood, the coach had come looking for him. Word about Aaron had gotten around. He was already six-foot-two, but more than that, he could *play*. So Coach Newey asked him to join the team, even though the season was well under way.

Now, out on the floor with the team for the first time, Aaron didn't want to show off, but he felt that he needed to prove that the coach hadn't done the wrong thing. And so he dribbled outside and canned another jumper. Then he drove toward the hoop and put in a left-handed lay-up. When he turned around, a short, dark-haired kid said, "You're like a machine. You don't miss."

"I miss plenty," Aaron said, suddenly embarrassed.

But the kid—Aaron heard someone call him Phil—said, "No one's going to beat us with you on our team."

"I don't know about that," Aaron mumbled, and he looked down at the floor.

"So are you this fantastic player who's really humble besides?"

Aaron's head popped up. But Phil was

laughing. And Aaron couldn't help smiling himself. "I'm a pretty good player," he said. "I only act like I'm humble."

"It's almost the same with me," Phil said. "I'm pretty humble. I only act like I can play."

Aaron laughed, and he felt himself relax a little.

But then he heard another voice, this one behind him. "He's a real hot shot, Phil. Can't you tell?"

Aaron turned around and looked at a guy about his same height—a boy with eyes that were almost hidden beneath a blunt forehead and big cheekbones.

Phil said, "He's the best thing that's happened to our team, Jared."

But Jared turned away. And Aaron knew what was going on. These guys had worked hard all fall and made the cut, and five of them had made the first team. Now some of them were asking themselves whether they were going to be benched to give a new guy room to play. This wasn't the first time Aaron had been through this.

Coach Newey blew his whistle. "Come over here, guys," he yelled, and he motioned the players to the bleachers. He was a big man, six-five or so, and solid. His voice was deep and round, but he spoke rather softly, and he seemed friendly with the boys.

When everyone piled into the seats, the coach said, "I guess you've met Aaron Reeves by now. I wouldn't usually bring a new guy in this time of year, but Aaron deserves a chance to play."

Aaron had sat down on the front row, and there were guys sitting on both sides of him. He tried to watch them out of the corners of his eyes, but he couldn't detect any reaction.

"Tell the players a little about yourself, Aaron," Coach Newey said.

Aaron sort of panicked. "Well...I just moved here."

"Where did you live before?"

"Bellingham, Washington." Aaron knew he ought to explain that he moved a lot, but he always got self-conscious when he talked to people he didn't know.

"Did you play a lot of ball up there?" the coach asked.

"Yeah. Well, sort of." He didn't want to get into the whole story. He had moved in after the season had started there, too. And even though he had only been a seventh grader, he had made the varsity team. But the truth was, that was only a small part of the time he put into the game. He spent many hours, every day, practicing by himself.

The coach seemed to sense that he wasn't going to get much out of Aaron. He stopped the questions.

But someone said, "What position did you play up there?"

"I've played all positions," Aaron said.

Aaron was tall enough to play either center or forward. But he preferred to play point guard. He liked to have the ball in his hands, and he liked being in control of a game.

Besides, he knew why the guy was asking. He was wondering whose spot Aaron was after.

The coach talked about the team the boys would be playing on Friday—the Tillamook Lumberjacks. He said the players were small but probably as quick as any they would play all season. "They really hustle on defense, too," he said. "We've got to make good passes, and we've got to take care of the ball."

Aaron had already found out that the team— the Greenwood Timber Wolves—had won only one game so far. And they had played six. But Aaron always believed his teams would

win. Since fourth grade every team he had
played on had done well. And Aaron had
always been the top scorer.

The coach had already given Aaron a little
booklet of plays that the Timber Wolves used
in the offense. It was pretty standard stuff—a
lot like the offense he had played in Bend,
Oregon, two years before.

But the coach had the players walk through
some of the plays, and he put Aaron at the
power forward spot. It didn't take long to see
that Aaron had caught on, and so the coach put
a defense on the floor.

Aaron made his cuts, set his screens, and at
first he passed off when he got the ball. He
didn't want the guys to think he was going to
be a ball hog. But his quickness was obvious.
Finally one time, when he slipped off a screen
and was all alone, he took a jump shot and
nailed it.

"Nice shot," Coach Newey said. "Now stop
just a minute. I want you kids to notice what
Aaron did right there." And then he gave a little speech about cutting close on a screen and
squaring up before taking a shot. "That's how
it's supposed to be done," he told the players.

And that's when Aaron heard it. Some guy

behind him whispered, not all that quietly, "Get used to the bench, Chris. You're going to be riding it soon."

And it must have been Chris who said, "Yeah. I think the coach already has his mind made up."

Aaron tried not to think about any of that. He would just do his best. If someone got knocked off the first team, he couldn't help it.

The coach had Aaron play with the first team for a long time. When he finally told Chris Jones to take over at power forward, he asked Aaron to switch to defense and cover him.

Aaron got on Chris like a shadow. He put a shoulder on him and tried to keep him off balance. Chris pushed back against the pressure.

That didn't bother Aaron. He only leaned harder on the guy. But it didn't take long to tell that Chris was frustrated. He shot his elbow out at Aaron a couple of times.

After a few more minutes, Chris finally erupted. He spun away from Aaron and gave him a shove. And then he turned toward the coach. "He's pushing me all over the place, Coach!" he shouted. "He can't do that."

The coach laughed. Then he said to Aaron, "You can't get away with quite that much contact in this league. But, Chris, that's what you'll have to get used to. In high school, the guys are going to put some flesh on you. That's the way the game is played."

Aaron was watching Chris. The guy was furious. He was not quite as tall as Aaron, but he was heavier. He could play tough himself if he made up his mind to do it. But he was a baby-faced kid, and he struck Aaron as someone who was accustomed to getting whatever he wanted.

Chris turned toward the player next to him— a guy named Darren. He was the small forward, a black kid who also had some good muscle on him. "Our new hot-shot player can't do any wrong, can he?" Chris said.

But Darren said, "Lay off, Chris," and then he gave Aaron a nod, as if to say, "Way to play."

When practice was over, Aaron showered and got dressed. Most of the guys took their time. Some of them had grouped together and were talking. Aaron thought about walking over to them and making some comment, just to break the ice a little. But it was very hard for him to do that sort of thing.

point guard, walked over to him. He had his shirt on, and he was buttoning it up. His hair was still wet and was sticking out in all directions. "My name's Phil Lewis," he said.

Aaron nodded. Then he reached down and pulled a shoe on and began to tighten the laces.

"How did you learn to shoot like that?"

Aaron knew better than to act humble again. "I just practice," he said.

"Someone told me you move a lot," Phil said. "How long are you going to be here?"

"I don't know. Less than a year, probably."

But in the next row of lockers, a voice said, "Sounds like a long time to me."

Phil looked embarrassed. "Don't let Chris bother you," he said.

"All I want to do is play some ball," Aaron said. And he told himself he didn't care what Chris—and some of the other guys—thought of him. But as he walked home, alone, he wished he could just stay in one place long enough for a team to accept him.

chapter two

Aaron did well at practice all week. And some of the guys, especially Phil, seemed excited to have him on the team. But he got the cold shoulder from Chris and Jared and some of the others.

So Aaron did what he usually did: he said very little and he played ball.

He didn't get very well acquainted at school either. Somehow, it always seemed too much work to develop friendships that would end so soon. And so he kept to himself most of the time. And when kids asked him questions about himself, he gave his usual short answers—and gave the impression that he didn't want to be bothered.

He did have his family, but he sometimes felt

alone at home, too. His dad worked long hours, often straight through weekends, and his mom was a rather quiet person herself. Greg, his little brother, was six years younger. He was a good little kid, but he was sort of self-contained himself.

Aaron could see that Phil Lewis was willing to become his friend. And Aaron tried to talk to him after practice each day. But trying to think of things to say was hard for Aaron— enough to send him home to his driveway, where he could shoot hoops by himself.

What he looked forward to was the first game. It was on the basketball floor that he felt in control and comfortable. And even though he would never have admitted it, it was there that he felt superior. He just always believed that he could outplay anyone who guarded him. And when he let a shot go, he expected it to go into the hoop.

When the game started, on Friday, Aaron was on the bench. But that didn't matter. He knew how these things worked. The coach had to let Chris, the regular starter, have some playing time before he let Aaron have his chance.

The game got off to a bad start for the Timber

Wolves, however. Jared got outjumped by the Lumberjacks' center, who was a good four inches shorter.

One of the Lumberjacks' guards grabbed the ball and knifed past his defender. He drove toward the hoop and then kicked the ball off to a trailer. The guy pulled up and hit the shot.

The Timber Wolves' guards brought the ball down the floor with defenders all over them. And Aaron could see immediately what the coach had meant about the Lumberjacks. They were hustlers—and quick. They were playing a tight man-to-man defense.

Phil tried to dribble past his defender, but he got cut off. He pulled up and looked to Shawn Whitesides, the other guard, and then he tried to pass to him. But the Lumberjack guard saw the pass coming all the way. He cut inside, took the pass as though it were intended for him, and dribbled to the hoop for the easy lay-up.

The game hadn't been going twenty seconds, and the Timber Wolves were down by four.

Things didn't get a whole lot better for the next couple of minutes either. Darren finally got hold of an offensive rebound off a missed shot by Chris, and he put it back up off the glass for the Timber Wolves' first basket. But by then the Lumberjacks were out in front, 6–2.

The Lumberjacks came back on offense. They had a good point guard—a boy named Watson—who could dribble past Phil without any problem.

Watson pushed the ball straight to the foul line. He faked a shot at the same time that his center rolled to the hoop. Jared took the fake and charged Watson. But Watson bounced a pass to the center, who was right under the basket. And it was another easy two.

Now the score was 8–2, and Aaron could see the Timber Wolves' fans giving up already. The game was at the Greenwood High School gym, across the street from the middle school, but only about a hundred of the students had bothered to come.

Aaron couldn't wait to get into the game. He loved to play against a man-to-man defense. He knew he had the moves to get past just about anyone, one-on-one.

Phil was still struggling to get the ball across the time line and into play. But the next time up the floor, he spotted Jared posting up near the foul line, and he shot a long pass to him.

Chris broke toward the hoop, got past his

man, and took a pass from Jared. He put up a
lay-up that rolled off the rim, no good.

But Jared grabbed the rebound and kicked it
back to Phil, at the top of the key. Phil was
open and he drained the shot.

So the score was 8–4, and now the Timber
Wolves needed to get rolling.

Aaron could see that the guy who was covering Chris—number fourteen—was the slowest
player on the Lumberjacks' team. Aaron knew
he could eat the guy up if he just got his
chance.

All the same, he was still on the bench—and
the time in the quarter was ticking away.

The Lumberjacks hurried the ball up the
court. Aaron watched number fourteen on offense. He understood his assignments. He
would hustle to the right spot, set his screens
or make his cuts. And he went hard to the
boards once a shot went up. But he wasn't con-
fident when he got the ball. For one thing, he
wouldn't dribble with his left hand.

But the Lumberjacks didn't need a lot of offense from their forwards. Once again, the
point guard passed to the center at the high
post, and then he broke past Phil and cut down
the middle. He took a return pass and drove all

the way to the hoop. He laid the ball up and in, and the score was 10–4.

Aaron needed to get into this game before the score got out of hand.

But the coach made no changes, and the quarter ended with the Lumberjacks up, 15–6. During the break between quarters, Aaron kept watching and waiting. Finally, the coach turned and said, "Aaron, check in. Go in for Chris."

Aaron jumped up and pulled his warmup jacket off. He ran to the scorer's table. This was it. This was the feeling he loved. He knew that he was going to make things happen, and he was going to enjoy every minute of it.

He couldn't help wondering how long it would take before the fans on both sides of the gym would be saying, "Who *is* that guy?"

But when play started again, Aaron could see that he still had a problem. He couldn't get the ball to the basket if the Timber Wolves couldn't get it up the floor.

The first time Phil tried to dribble, the Lumberjacks' guard stripped him clean. Then he broke to the other hoop and scored. So now the Timber Wolves were down, 17–6.

Aaron knew he had to help. He worked his

way up the floor, and when Phil got in trouble again, he ran toward him. "Over here," he called, and Phil tossed the ball to him.

Aaron took the pass, turned, and dribbled straight at his defender. The guy got ready, but Aaron faked right, dribbled behind his back, and then cut left.

He broke toward the foul line, but the big center came out to stop him. Aaron faked the guy into the air and then went up for a soft jumper that arched high and dropped through the net.

Yes!

Aaron could feel it. He had the touch.

He hustled back and covered his man, but he stayed a little too loose. He wanted number fourteen to get the ball outside.

And he did.

As soon as the forward took the pass, Aaron faced him. He stayed on the guy's right side and dared him to go left. But the forward tried to go right anyway, and Aaron's quick hand shot out and knocked the ball away.

Aaron chased the ball down and grabbed it himself. The players took off the other way, and Phil called for the ball. Aaron passed off to him, but he didn't hurry to the front court. He stayed with the guards and made sure they got the ball across the time line. Phil managed all right this time, however, and then he passed into the corner to Darren.

Aaron hustled to his position and waited for the play to develop. Darren passed to Jared on the post, but the hustling defense cut off the passing lanes. Jared was trapped. Aaron suddenly broke toward the key, leaving his defender behind. Jared spotted him and hit him with a pass.

Aaron saw the center come at him again. He took the ball out of the air with one hand and spun as he put it on the floor the first time. Then he switched hands and broke under the center's outstretched arms. He laid the ball up with a little one-handed finger-roll shot.

And it went in.

He turned, took a couple of steps, then suddenly threw on the brakes and cut back toward the guards. And he caught them making a sloppy pass. He stole the ball and drove straight to the hoop. He was tempted to go for the slam dunk, but he held himself back. He put up a simple lay-up, and now he had cut the lead to five.

The crowd was suddenly excited. He could

hear the Greenwood kids really whooping it up. He heard some guy yell, "Way to go, number twelve." His own fans didn't even know his name yet.

Aaron could see that the Lumberjacks were rattled a little. He heard their point guard yell, "All right, you guys. Settle down." Then he held up his fist, signaling a play.

Aaron covered his man, staying off him a little, watching to help his teammates on defense. The pass went to the center, who turned and put up a jumper. The ball banged high off the rim.

Aaron charged the hoop, and he skied high. He outjumped everyone and came down with the ball. Then he took off toward the other basket, dribbling the ball himself.

Defenders were dropping back fast, but Aaron kept driving. He slipped into the key, hesitated as though he were going to stop, then darted to the hoop again. As he went up for the lay-up, Watson jumped with him.

In the air, Aaron switched the ball to his left hand and reversed to the left side of the hoop for his lay-up. Watson clubbed him hard, but Aaron still got the ball up and in.

The whistle sounded. The score was now

17–14. And Aaron had a foul shot coming.

But now the Lumberjacks' coach was yelling, "Time out!"

Aaron had expected that.

chapter three

When Aaron and his teammates ran off the floor, their fans were all standing, cheering—going nuts. "Way to go, Reeves!" someone shouted. They were finding out his name.

The coach was the only one who didn't seem excited. "Okay, kids, nice comeback," he told them, but then he talked about running the plays on offense. Finally, he looked at Aaron. "You took them by surprise," he said. "But now they'll be looking for you. So lay off the freelance stuff and work with the offense."

Aaron nodded and said, "Okay," but he was a little annoyed. The coach could have given him a little more credit for what he had done.

It was Phil who slapped Aaron on the back

and said, "Way to go. You were *amazing*."

But Aaron was watching the other guys. Chris was standing quietly, his hands tucked into the pockets of his warmup jacket. And just before the players walked back on the court, he said something to Jared. Aaron heard Jared say, "Yeah, sure—if I ever get to touch the ball again."

Aaron couldn't believe it. Would the guy really rather lose than let Aaron take the shots?

He told himself not to care, not to worry about it. He would win this game whether he was playing with a bunch of losers or not. He looked up at the bleachers and noticed that his mom was sitting near the top. He hadn't noticed her before, but he didn't think she'd been there the whole time. She gave him a smile and waved her fist, as if to say, "Go get 'em!"

Aaron made the foul shot and then ran back on defense. But when the center missed a shot and Jared took the rebound, Aaron saw that the Lumberjacks were falling back quickly and setting up a zone defense. No surprise there.

Phil wasn't being pressed anymore, and so Aaron ran down the floor and took up his position on the right side. Immediately, two defenders came out to cover him. Obviously, the whole idea was to keep him from getting the ball.

That meant the rest of the defense had to cover the Timber Wolves three-on-four, but the Lumberjacks seemed willing to take that chance.

Aaron played it cool for the moment. He stayed outside as much as he could, pulling the defense with him. That opened things up in the middle, but Shawn got a wide open shot and missed it.

Jared went up for the rebound, but one of the Lumberjacks' guards hustled inside and took the ball out of his hands just as he came down with it.

The Lumberjacks pushed the ball back up the floor, and Aaron hassled them a little. But they made good passes and they got the ball to the forecourt and then to their center. The guy Aaron was covering stayed wide, keeping Aaron outside, and the play went to the other side of the court.

The Lumberjacks' small forward cut off a screen and got the pass. He took a shot and missed, but the center crashed for the rebound. Aaron was coming hard, too, but he got there an instant too late. The center laid the ball in, and Aaron caught him on the arm for a foul.

The center put the shot in, and suddenly the lead was back to six, 20–14. Aaron could feel the momentum switch, and he knew he had to do something—no matter what the coach had told him.

Aaron ran to the other end of the floor and took up his position. But then, just as Phil brought the ball into the forecourt, Aaron broke toward him, getting a step on both his defenders. And Phil passed the ball to him.

Aaron caught the ball and stopped. He faked a pass, then broke forward, trying to split the two defenders.

They reacted quickly, however, so Aaron pulled up and took a long jump shot. But this time he missed. The ball was on target, but just a little short.

Aaron didn't worry about that. He knew what he could do. But as he ran back the other way, he saw Chris getting up from the bench, pulling his warmup jacket off. Aaron couldn't believe it. That was the first shot he had missed.

At the other end of the floor, Jared fouled the Lumberjacks' center. As soon as play stopped, Chris trotted onto the floor and told

Aaron, "I'm back in for you."

Aaron was mad. He ran to the sidelines and was about to sit on the bench, well away from the coach, but the coach called him over. Aaron grabbed his warmup jacket and slipped it on, then he sat down by the coach.

"Aaron," Coach Newey said, "you're a whole lot better than anyone out there. But you can't do it by yourself. We have to work as a team. When I put you back in, I want you to run the plays and pass the ball."

Aaron didn't say a word. He hunched over and looked at the floor. Coaches were all alike. They would rather run their plays and lose than let someone dominate the game. Aaron could win this game if the coach would only let him.

All the same, he was on the bench, and that's where he stayed the rest of the half. At halftime, the coach gave pretty much the same little speech, about working the ball, passing—the whole business. But the stupid thing was, the Lumberjacks were up by ten points again, 32–22, and it could have been worse. The Lumberjacks had turned cold and had missed a lot of open shots. But they were controlling the game.

As the players took their warmup shots before the second half started, Aaron could hear kids from his school yelling, "Put number twelve back in!" Or, "Hey, Coach, play Reeves!"

Aaron figured that wouldn't help much. He had never met a coach who liked to be told what to do.

And so the third quarter went pretty much the way the end of the first half had gone. The Lumberjacks built their lead to fourteen, and their coach started playing more of their second-team players. With some of those guys in the game, the Timber Wolves came back a little, getting the lead down to ten again.

But Aaron, and everyone else in the gym, knew that the Timber Wolves' only hope was to put Aaron back in. And finally, halfway through the third quarter, the coach did just that.

Aaron knew he had to be careful. He couldn't start gunning from everywhere. He had to play the offense, pass off, and satisfy the coach.

And that's what he tried to do. The defense went back to the zone, and they double-covered him again. Still, he was quick enough to get open at times. But when he drove to the hoop, he pulled the defense around him and then hit open teammates.

The problem was, his teammates kept missing easy shots. He would dish the ball to big Jared, right under the basket, and the guy would bang the ball off the rim or fumble it away before he even got the shot off.

It was frustrating. Aaron missed a couple of shots himself, but he also hit some, and he rebounded like a wild man at both ends of the court. He put back a couple of missed shots by his teammates, and he kept the Lumberjacks from getting second shots on their end of the court.

Gradually, the Timber Wolves were sneaking back into the game. At the end of the third quarter, the score was 42–35.

And then, just as the fourth quarter began, Aaron dribbled to the baseline with two defenders all over him. He spotted Darren in the corner and hit him with a bounce pass. Darren was all alone, but he hurried his shot anyway, and it was long, clear over the basket.

All Aaron could think was that he should have taken the jumper from the baseline, two guys on him or not. At least he would have gotten a good shot off. And maybe he would have canned it and gotten the lead down to five.

Aaron knew he was going to have to take over, if his team was going to win.

He got back on defense, but he sagged away from his man. The guy just wasn't that dangerous. When a pass came into the guy playing center, Aaron slipped into the middle, double-teamed him, and took him by surprise. The center shuffled his feet and got called for traveling.

Aaron ran to the sideline, got the ball from the ref, and he passed it in. He moved down the floor with the guards. As Phil neared the top of the key, Aaron darted past him and Phil fed him the ball.

It was a freelance move, but it caught the defense by surprise. Aaron took two dribbles, driving hard, and then pulled up. The defense was still dropping back. Aaron squared up and fired a jump shot that split the net.

Now he had the feel. No one could stop him. He knew it.

For the next several minutes, he worked hard at both ends of the floor. His quickness got him position; his jumping ability put him above everyone in the air. He grabbed off rebounds; he made great passes. And he didn't miss a shot. He made every point for the Timber Wolves, and he brought them even and then ahead of the Lumberjacks.

With two minutes to go, he hit a three-pointer, and his team was up by five. It was an amazing run, and the fans on both sides were all standing and screaming.

Aaron knew that no one could stop him now.

But the whistle sounded. The Lumberjacks wanted time out. Aaron ran to the sidelines. He could hear the Greenwood fans shouting his name. Everyone seemed to know it now.

Phil and Shawn were pounding him on the back.

But the coach was telling everyone to be quiet, and then he said, "Okay, kids, I want you to go into the spread offense and take some time off the clock. Aaron, you haven't practiced the spread, so I'm putting Chris back in."

Aaron was stunned. He stared back at the coach, letting his eyes express his rage. But he said nothing.

When the players ran onto the court, Aaron put on his jacket and sat down. Jerry McKinny, one of the subs on the bench, said to him, "He should have left you in," but Aaron didn't respond. He just watched, and waited for the disaster.

But Watson took a long shot that missed, and Phil was in the right place to get the long rebound. He turned to dribble and got fouled. And he hit his foul shots.

And that's how the last two minutes went. The Lumberjacks were a little too desperate to score and were forcing shots. And the Timber Wolves, in their spread offense, kept drawing fouls. Shawn missed a couple of shots, but Phil hit three of four in the final minute, and the Timber Wolves hung on for the win, 59–55.

Aaron was surprised that the other guys had pulled it off, and he was still a little mad at the coach. But he had gotten the win, and that was what mattered most.

When the buzzer sounded, he ran onto the floor and congratulated the guys—especially Phil.

Phil was grinning. "Hey, I'm a hero," he said. "Tell me how to act humble. I've never had to do it before."

But the students were spilling onto the floor now, and it was Aaron, not Phil, who was getting all the attention.

chapter four

Aaron was not very comfortable with everyone crowded around him. Kids were slapping him on the back and shouting to him, congratulating him.

Aaron didn't really say anything. He nodded, over and over, and kept trying to walk away. Some of the players had come toward him, too, but they couldn't get near him.

"You're a one-man team," one guy yelled.

Aaron glanced at Shawn, who was standing closest to him. He saw the reaction on his face. Shawn shot an angry look at the kid who had yelled, not at Aaron, but then he walked away.

Aaron tried to catch up, but he got slowed down by the crowd. When Aaron finally made it to the locker room, the players were celebrating. But he had the feeling that Shawn had told everyone what the guy outside had said. Almost everyone told him he had played a great game, but Aaron didn't sense a lot of excitement in their voices.

And Chris had already showered. He was talking to Jared while he was getting dressed. Neither one of them said a word to Aaron.

Aaron told himself he didn't care. He walked over to his own locker. But Phil followed. "Hey, I need your phone number," he said, grinning.

"What for?" Aaron asked.

"I'm going to start selling it," he said. "All the girls want it. Robin Pemberton was just telling me how *cute* you are." And then he did a little imitation. " 'He's *soooo* tall. And he's got that dreamy look in his eyes all the time.' "

Aaron couldn't handle that. He headed for the shower. But when he got back, Phil was still in his uniform, the green cloth soaked dark with sweat, and he was still talking. But he was more serious now. "Man, I wish we'd had you all season," he told Aaron. "No one would have beaten us. Have you ever played on a losing team?"

Aaron shrugged. "I don't know. Not really."

But Jared walked by just at that moment. And he stopped. "What do you mean, 'team'?" he said. "Just feed him the ball and he'll do all the shooting."

The room was suddenly silent.

"Lay off, Jared," Phil said.

Aaron took a long look at Jared. He thought of some things to say, but he held his tongue. And Jared walked away.

So Aaron dressed quickly, wanting to get out of the locker room. But the coach came up to him. "Aaron, you played a heck of a game," he said.

"Thanks," Aaron said, but he heard the hesitancy in the coach's voice, and he knew something else was coming.

"You do need to work with our offense a little better. We're not going anywhere, in the long run, if we rely too much on one guy."

Aaron glanced around and saw that everyone was watching—and listening.

"Okay," Aaron said.

He sat down and pulled his shoes on, and he kept his head down to tie them—as the coach walked away. Aaron couldn't believe he could work that hard, pull off the win, and get halfway chewed out for it.

He grabbed his stuff and got out of there.

When Aaron got home, he went straight to his room. He could hear his little brother playing video games, and he knew his mother was in the house somewhere. But he didn't want to talk to her right now.

All the same, in a few minutes she knocked at his door and then peeked in. "Nice game," she said.

"Thanks."

"What's wrong?"

"Nothing."

"Don't give me that, Aaron. I know when something's wrong with you." She leaned against the door frame and smiled at him. She was a tall woman, with light hair and surprisingly dark brown eyes—just like Aaron. Aaron could talk with her better than with anyone, but he still didn't feel like talking now.

"Mom, I said I'm okay."

"Fine. But let me tell you what happened. It's not that hard to guess."

"I told you, I—"

"The players weren't that thrilled about the

new guy coming in and stealing the show. Right?"

Aaron didn't say anything.

"Isn't that right?"

"Yeah, I guess. That's part of it."

"What's the rest?"

"The coach chewed me out, too. He said I've got to *play with the offense.*"

"What's wrong with that?"

"Mom, if one guy can shoot better than the others, he ought to do the shooting. That isn't that hard to figure out."

"Really good teams always have more balance than that, Aaron. You know that as well as I do."

"Really good teams have more than one good player. But if that's all you've got, you better go with it."

"And then how do the other players learn?"

Aaron decided he wanted out of this debate. His mom had played basketball in college, so she thought she knew all about it. But she had listened to too much of the stuff that coaches always said.

"Aaron, I see what you're going to do all over again. You'll pull all the more into yourself, outplay your teammates, and be the best player in the whole league—and perfectly miserable."

"I'm not miserable."

"Right. You do look awfully cheery right now."

"Someday, when I'm in the NBA, these guys will want my autograph."

Mom didn't like that. He heard that little clucking sound she made with her tongue sometimes—her sound of disgust.

"Aaron, that's just dandy. I hope you make it. But if you get there without any friends, how happy are you going to be?"

Suddenly Aaron sat up. "It's not my fault, Mom. I just do my best. It's those guys who don't like me. And they don't even know me."

"And Aaron, they never will. Because you won't let them."

Now Aaron was mad. Mom really didn't understand what it was like. If he were a mediocre player, he could have plenty of friends, but being as good as he was, all he got was jealousy and rejection. Well, fine. He could live with it.

Mom tried to get him to talk after that, but Aaron clammed up. He wasn't going to have this conversation again. He and his mom had been through it too many times before.

Finally, she gave up and left.

At practice, all the next week, Aaron worked extremely hard. And he made sure he "played with the offense." Then he went home after the team workout each night and practiced on his own. The house his family was renting had a hoop on the front of the garage. Aaron had rigged up a floodlight so he could see well enough to practice after dark.

It was cold and damp outside—and the driveway was cracked and hard to dribble on. But he didn't care. He took fifty foul shots every night. And he shot jumpers in a circle, from every angle around the perimeter. He worked on his fancy lay-ups and slams, too—the ones that guys on the team would call "hot dog shots" if he were to try them at practice.

When he finally went inside, he did his homework, but quickly, and with little interest. He cared about grades in a way. He knew he had to have decent grades to get recruited by the best colleges. But he figured it was his playing that would count the most, and his grades didn't have to be all that great.

• • •

The next game was an "away" game in the little town of Chester. The team was called the Panthers. The Timber Wolves had lost to them by a fairly one-sided score a few weeks before.

But this time something was different. When the coach announced the starting lineup, Aaron was playing at the power forward spot. Chris didn't look surprised, but he didn't look pleased, either.

As Aaron got ready to run out onto the floor, the coach took hold of his arm and said, "Aaron, remember. Don't try to do it by yourself."

Aaron agreed to that. But the game got started a lot the way practice had gone all week. Aaron found the open guy and got the ball to him—only to watch the ball bounce off the rim, or miss entirely.

His rebounding, his shooting, his defense—all were keeping the team in the game. But at the end of the first quarter, the score was 16–11, with the Panthers on top.

Aaron was frustrated, but he vowed to himself that he would play the game the way the coach wanted it. He just had to turn up his play another notch and hope he could make the difference without shooting so much that he got the coach mad.

During the break between quarters, Coach Newey asked Aaron to switch over and guard the small forward. "He's scoring all the points for those guys. You've got the speed to stay with him. Let's see you shut him down."

Aaron was excited to do just that. The player's name was Johnson, and Phil had told Aaron that he was one of the best players the Timber Wolves had played all year. He was a black kid who had grown up playing in big-city leagues in Portland. And Aaron could see that he was good—but he still thought he could stop him.

Aaron got tough on defense, all right, and maybe a little too aggressive. When he put his hand on Johnson's back and tried to keep him from moving toward the hoop, the whistle sounded.

"Number twelve, you're pushing the man," the ref shouted.

And so Aaron backed off a little for a time. But a couple of minutes later, Johnson went up for a jumper and Aaron leaped with him. He thought he made a perfect block, but the referee blew the whistle and called him for another foul.

Aaron didn't complain. He just told himself that he had to be more careful. But it was too late. The coach obviously didn't want him to get another foul before halftime. He sent Chris into the game.

And that's when the Panthers began to build their lead.

chapter five

By halftime the Panthers were ahead, 36–19. And Aaron could tell that the players had given up. Aaron was probably the only one in the gym who still believed the Timber Wolves could win. But the coach had to let him play— *really* play.

"Okay," the coach told the players. "I'm putting Aaron back in the lineup. Let's set some good screens for him and get him some shots. These kids still don't know what he can do—and they aren't doubling him yet."

Aaron couldn't believe it. The coach was coming to his senses. Aaron was going to show some people some *hoops* now. The coach had given him permission.

As the second half started, Phil followed instructions. The first time the Timber Wolves set up their offense, he started a rotation play to the right side—one that set a pick for Aaron.

Aaron came off the screen clean, and he got off a nice shot, but it didn't go down.

Aaron didn't worry about that. The shot had felt good, and now he just had to get in the motion again.

And so the next time down the floor, the Timber Wolves ran the same play, and this time Aaron got the shot again, a jumper from just right of the key. He popped the ball in the net, and that was the start.

He came alive on defense, too. He didn't push Johnson as hard as he had before, but he stayed right with him. He kept the ball from him most of the time, stole a couple of passes, and made life miserable for him when he did get the ball.

He was taking the Panthers' best shooter out of the game, all by himself, and at the other end of the floor, he was hitting most of his shots.

With the score now 40–29, Aaron charged toward Phil, just as he crossed the ten-second line. He took a pass and then turned and faced

Johnson. He faked left, dribbled right, then drove hard again.

Johnson reacted quickly, staying with him, and so Aaron pulled up and took the jump shot. Johnson jumped with him and tried to block the shot, but he slapped Aaron across the arm.

The shot went in, off the glass, and the whistle sounded. Aaron finished off the three-point play, and suddenly the score was 40–32. The Timber Wolves, who had seemed dead, were back in the game. They still had a shot.

But the whistle sounded again. The Panthers were calling time out.

As Aaron walked off the floor, he looked up at the clock. There were three minutes left in the third quarter. He had plenty of time. He was going to win this game.

But he guessed what the coach would be saying. And he was right. "You know what the Panthers' coach is saying right now, kids. He's telling them to get all over number twelve."

Phil laughed. "I heard one of their players say, 'Who *is* that guy?'"

The coach smiled, too, but he said, "Listen, guys, they're going to start doubling up on him now, and that means someone else is going to be open. Let's get some lay-ups, and let's show these kids we can play as a team."

As the boys walked back to the court, Phil said to Aaron, "If they go into a zone defense, they'll probably cover you and cover the middle but leave me alone. I can hit from outside. Look for me at the top of the key, and I'll see if I can get some three-pointers."

Aaron hesitated, but then he said, "Phil, don't take this wrong, but I'm a better outside shooter than you are. If they go to the zone, they might not double me if I stay way outside. Get the ball to me and let *me* hit the threes."

Phil began to say something but stopped himself. And then he nodded, as though he knew Aaron was right.

Aaron sort of wished he could take back the words. But he knew he was right. If Phil started throwing up air balls from the outside, the Timber Wolves were dead.

And so the first time Phil brought the ball into the forecourt on offense, he dribbled to the right side. Sure enough, the Panthers were in a zone. Aaron drifted away from the basket, pulling only one man with him.

Phil hit Aaron with a pass. Aaron pumped

up a three-pointer and hit it.

The score was 40–35.

But the Panthers' coach was yelling to his players not to give "number twelve" any more shots. And Coach Newey was yelling to Aaron to "move the ball around."

Aaron figured he better not take another shot for a while—at least nothing that long.

The Panthers hurried the ball up the court. The Timber Wolves hustled back, however, so the Panthers set up their half-court offense and tried to work for a good shot. But the center got called for a three-second violation, and the Timber Wolves were back in business.

The Panthers were putting some full-court pressure on Phil now. He passed off to Shawn and then took a pass back. The two of them got the ball up the court without much trouble.

The Panthers settled back into their zone. Aaron stayed outside, but this time two guys went with him. Phil spotted Darren by himself on the left side and got the ball to him.

Darren took the pass and drove to the hoop, but the Panther zone adjusted quickly and cut him off. The guy was just too slow. He tossed the ball back out front to Phil, and Phil tried to feed it underneath to Jared.

But the pass had some zing on it, and it slipped through Jared's hands and rolled out of bounds.

The Panthers tossed the ball in, and the guard pushed it up the court. Then he dropped it off to his power forward, who was running alongside him. The forward went straight to the hoop and in for the lay-up. But Aaron came flying through the air and slammed the ball away.

Aaron was sure he had a clean block, but the referee didn't think so. He called Aaron for the foul, and the next thing Aaron knew, he was sitting on the bench again.

"Take a rest for a couple of minutes," the coach said. "I don't want you to get another foul before the fourth quarter. We're going to need you at the end."

Aaron didn't say anything, but he thought the coach was all wrong. Aaron knew how to be careful. He wouldn't foul out. And the team was going to lose what they had gained out there, with him on the bench.

But that's where he sat the rest of the quarter, and the Panthers did rebuild their lead a little. The score was 47–37 when the fourth quarter started and Aaron got back in the game.

And now Aaron knew he had to get another run going.

Right off the bat, Phil got the ball to him in the corner, and Aaron lofted another three-pointer. But this one was just a little short. It hit the rim and bounced high. The Panthers grabbed the rebound, and Coach Newey yelled, "Work the ball inside, Aaron. Find the open man."

But Aaron knew better. He would make that shot next time. And if he hadn't been sitting down so long and gotten cold, he wouldn't have missed the last one.

Aaron had to get the ball back. He watched the Panthers' point guard, and he decoyed a little, staying back from Johnson. When the guard looked where he was going to pass and didn't really snap the ball, Aaron darted in front of Johnson and stole the pass.

Aaron dribbled hard into the forecourt with the point guard running with him. He went all the way to the hoop and in for the lay-up. The guard hit him hard, trying to stop the shot, but Aaron hung onto the ball and then flipped it up after he had taken the collision.

The ball bounced off the glass and into the basket. And Aaron had a foul shot coming besides. He put that in, too, for the three-point play, and the lead was down to seven.

And now Aaron didn't run back up the court. "Help me, Phil," he yelled. "Let's pressure them." And so without the coach's instructions, the two doubled on the guard as the ball came in.

The guard grabbed the inbounds pass, but he was trapped. He tried to spin and he dragged his pivot foot. The ref called him for traveling, and just like that, the Timber Wolves had the ball back.

Aaron passed the ball into Phil, then ran inbounds and called for the ball back. Phil hit him in the corner again, and Aaron fired another long bomb.

Swish!

And now the ten-point lead was down to four. Aaron was going to get these guys.

But the coach was yelling to him again.

Aaron knew he had to feed the ball to someone else and hope for the best. But the next three times down the floor, his teammates missed shots, and the Panthers scored on an easy lay-up when Jared let his man get away.

It was maddening to Aaron. Time was running down. Three minutes to play, and now the lead was back to six. His only chance was to hog the ball, whether the coach liked it or not.

And so he waited with the guards, asked for the ball and got it, and then drove into the forecourt himself. And once there, he dribbled to the side of the key, gave a fake, and then did a three-sixty spin that shook his defender. Another guy was on him by then, but Aaron switched hands on the dribble and busted past him and straight to the hoop.

When the center came at him, Aaron slipped under the basket and put up a reverse lay-up, with plenty of spin on the ball. The ball came off the glass with some English on it and rolled into the net.

It was an incredible shot, and the crowd went nuts.

Not all that many kids had made the trip to Chester from Greenwood, but they were into the game now. The lead was back to four, and the fans could feel that Aaron was going to pull off another win.

chapter six

Aaron knew he had to make something happen on defense again. He couldn't let the Panthers score. He hassled the point guard in backcourt, but the guy didn't rattle.

The coach was yelling for Aaron to get back. And Aaron knew he had to. He hurried down the court and picked up his man, and he watched him closely. But he was also looking for a chance for a steal.

He figured the Panthers would try to get the ball to Johnson. And they did.

When the point guard fired the pass, Aaron stepped in and tried to intercept. He was an instant late. But Johnson had to reach, and he was off balance as he caught the ball. Before he could dribble, Aaron reached in and ripped the ball loose.

Shawn was right there to pick the ball up. He tossed it to Phil, and the Timber Wolves took off toward their basket.

Aaron didn't take any chances. He ran with Phil, taking up a lane outside him. When Phil got cut off and had to pull up, Aaron yelled, "Here! Right here!"

Phil flipped the ball to him, and Aaron drove to the hoop. Johnson was right with him, expecting Aaron to go all the way in again. So Aaron stopped and gunned the jumper.

Swish, again.

Two points. The lead was cut in half.

Aaron glanced at the clock. Just over a minute to go. He couldn't let the Panthers score. He had to get the ball back again.

He worked on the point guard and tried to make the steal, but he couldn't pull it off. And so he charged back to Johnson. But now he was guessing that the guard would be careful and try to stay away from Aaron's quick defensive moves.

The Panthers could run most of the time out. The coach was yelling for them to work the ball, to keep it moving.

Aaron could hear the crowd roaring, and inside was that knowledge that never left him—that he was the best player on the floor. He was the one who had to make something happen.

Coach Newey was yelling not to foul. And Aaron knew that he was right. But they couldn't give up a score either.

He watched one of the guards dribble the ball out front toward the right side. Suddenly Aaron rushed at him, doubling him, trapping him in the corner near the ten-second line.

And the kid panicked. He tried to lob a pass back to the point guard, and he lofted it too high. Phil leaped and deflected the ball away from the guard. Then he grabbed it and tried to drive down the floor.

But Phil wasn't all that fast, and the Panthers got back quickly. Once in forecourt, he had to slow things up. And then the coach yelled to him to call time out. Phil turned to the ref and shouted, "Time!"

Aaron looked at the clock. Thirty-eight seconds. Two points would tie the score. But three would win the game.

The coach didn't see it that way. "Let's get an easy bucket and stay alive. A three-pointer is a low-percentage shot."

And so he designed the play. He told Phil to take some time off the clock. And then, when the coach yelled to him to go, Aaron should break to the outside, as though he wanted to take the three-pointer. That should pull two defenders away from the basket.

Phil should fake to that side, and then hit Jared at the high post. Jared should either roll to the hoop or pass off. Somebody had to be open.

True. But Aaron also knew that Jared was just as likely to dribble the ball off his foot—or miss the lay-up.

Aaron wanted the ball. In three-point range. If he could get the shot, he could win this thing right now.

But he did what the coach told him. He waited for Phil to use up some time, and then, when the coach yelled, Aaron broke to the outside.

When he looked back, however, Phil was in trouble. He hadn't gotten the pass off. Two guards had charged Phil and had him trapped.

Aaron dashed toward Phil, and Phil slipped a bounce pass to him. It was better than Aaron could have hoped. He had his shot.

He dribbled to the three-point line, pushing his defenders back. Then he pulled up. He went straight up, smooth, and the shot felt perfect.

The ball arched toward the basket, right on line.

Aaron threw his hands in the air before it

hit the net. He knew it was in.

But no.

It was just a shade long. It hit the back of the rim and bounced away. The Panthers controlled the rebound and the game was over.

The Timber Wolves had lost.

Aaron couldn't believe he had missed. He had *known* he could make that shot. And it had looked so perfect.

He stood on the court with his hands on his hips, still staring at the basket. And that's when Jared charged toward him. "What were you thinking?" he yelled. "I was wide open under the basket. All you had to do was hit me."

Somewhere in Aaron's consciousness was an awareness that Jared was right. Jared had been there, his arms up, waiting. But Aaron had never even thought of passing off.

He turned away from Jared and started to walk toward the locker room.

"You think you can do it all alone," Jared was yelling at him. "You're good. But you're not half as good as you think you are."

Aaron knew what he wanted to say: "Half as good as I think I am is still twice as good as you." But he didn't say that or anything else. He just walked off the floor.

Some of the Greenwood fans told him, "Great game." One guy even said, "The coach should have left you in the whole game. You could have won it."

Aaron didn't say anything to the guy, but he believed it, too.

And yet, he knew something else. And he didn't know how to deal with it. He should have made that pass. Why hadn't he?

He was the first one in the showers, the first one dressed. But that didn't help him because he couldn't leave. He had to ride back with all the other players.

And so he slipped away to a distant corner of the locker room. He sat and stared straight ahead. He didn't want to talk to anyone.

The other players weren't saying much either. But he knew what they were thinking. They had all heard what Jared said. They all agreed.

When Aaron felt a hand on his shoulder, he looked up and saw the coach. "Well, did you learn something today?" Coach Newey asked.

Aaron wasn't going to say it, not what the coach wanted to hear. "I don't know," he mumbled.

"Why did you take that shot when I had already told you not to?"

"I thought I could make it."

"That's right. And you almost did. But I told you it was a poor-percentage shot. I told you to look for the open man and get the easy two. There was Jared waving his arms under the basket, wide open, and all you had to do was make the pass."

Aaron wanted to say, "Yeah, and he probably would have blown it." But he couldn't say that. Not after missing the shot himself.

"Listen, Aaron, I've coached this game for a long time. And there's one thing I know. It takes five guys working together to make a good team. But you—you trust only yourself."

Aaron knew that was true, and he even knew that he was wrong, in a way. But when had these guys done anything to earn any trust? And besides, what would Coach Newey be saying right now if he had hit the shot? Other coaches had always seemed ready to forgive him for hogging the ball if his team got the win.

But Coach Newey seemed to know that's what Aaron was thinking. "One guy, working by himself—if he's good enough—can take over a game at times. He can get some wins that way. But in the long run, it doesn't work."

Aaron had heard that kind of stuff a thousand times. Maybe it was even true. But he just couldn't help it. When it came right down to it, he really did trust himself more than anyone he had ever played with.

The coach seemed to think things over for a time, and then he said, "I'm not going to start you in the next game, Aaron. I'm going to start a *team*. And then, when you get in the game, if you want to be part of that team, fine. If not, you can stay on the bench. Or turn in your uniform."

Aaron didn't say a word. But somewhere in the room, he heard someone say, "Good. That's what he deserves."

Chris.

And then another voice—Jared's—said, "That's right."

Aaron came close to exploding. He almost stood up and screamed, "Yeah, and where would you guys be without me? You would have lost by twenty points instead of two."

But as usual, he sat still and stared straight ahead. And the coach walked away.

chapter seven

On the bus, on the way back to Greenwood, Aaron kept to himself. Most of the players sat in the first few seats, but Aaron walked to the back and sat by himself. He stared out the window and ignored the other players.

By the time the bus was under way, he could hear the players already laughing and goofing around. He knew the game hadn't meant half as much to them as it had to him.

What a bunch of losers!

It didn't matter to them if Aaron spent the rest of the season on the bench—and they lost *all* their games.

Greenwood was only about fifteen miles away, and so it wasn't a long trip. But about halfway home, Phil got up from his seat, walked to the back of the bus, and sat down next to Aaron.

"Are you okay?" he asked.

"Sure," Aaron said, and he tried to sound final. He didn't want to talk.

"I think the coach should have said one other thing."

Aaron didn't ask what it was. He figured Phil would say it, whether he asked or not.

"He should have told you that we wouldn't have been anywhere close to those guys if you hadn't played so well. You've made the team twice as good as it used to be."

"Thanks," Aaron said, and he felt the anger in him quiet just a little.

"According to Robin, you make the team twice as good-looking, too. But I don't know. As soon as I get my growth spurt, she's going to start noticing who the real stud is."

But Aaron wasn't ready to kid around.

When the bus parked at the middle school, Phil waited and got off with Aaron. "Where do you live?" he asked.

Aaron pointed across town. "Over on Pine Street."

"Oh, yeah? I kind of live that way. Are you walking?"

"Yeah."

"I'll walk with you."

And so the two walked together, cutting across the little downtown area and then past some old frame houses that had been there since the town was built. Pine Street was in a newer area, where some of the nicest homes were.

"What do you think of Greenwood?" Phil asked as the boys neared Aaron's house. The sun was going down, and it was getting cold outside. Phil had zipped up his jacket and tucked his hands in his pockets.

Aaron hadn't said too much on the way home. Phil had worked to keep a conversation going. "It's okay, I guess," Aaron said. "I don't pay too much attention to where we live."

"It sounds kind of fun to move all the time," Phil said. "I've lived right here all my life. And I've hardly been anywhere. The only big city I've seen is Portland."

"You haven't missed anything," Aaron said.

"So are you like this really angry young man—because you've had such a rough childhood?" Phil grinned.

Aaron tried not to smile, but he couldn't

help himself. "Yeah. That's me," he said.

"You wouldn't beat me up or anything, would you?"

"No. I don't want to get locked up for child abuse."

"Hey, when I get that growth spurt, I'm going to be bigger than you. So watch out."

Aaron stopped. "This is where I live," he said, and he expected Phil to say good-bye.

Instead, Phil said, "Do you have a minute to show me something?"

"Yeah. I guess."

"I've watched you dribble behind your back. I keep trying, but I can't do it."

"I'll show you." Aaron walked to the side of his garage, crouched, and plugged in the cord to the floodlight. Then he walked inside the garage and came back with a ball.

Aaron's spirits rose as he and Phil worked together. There was something sort of satisfying about trying to put into words what he had done only by instinct up until now.

And Phil began to get the idea.

After a while, Aaron said, "I've got this video of NBA highlights—all the big stars doing these amazing things with the ball.

That's one way I try to learn."

"I'd like to see that."

"We can go in and watch it now if you want."

So the two walked inside, and Aaron introduced Phil to his mother. She wanted to know how the game had gone. But Aaron only said, "We lost," and then he and Phil went to Aaron's room. He didn't want to think about the game anymore.

Phil couldn't believe that Aaron had his own TV, but Aaron said he hardly ever watched it. He was always outside practicing.

"It sounds as if you spend most of your time alone," Phil said.

"Yeah, I do."

"How come?"

Aaron had put the video in the machine, and he was holding the remote in his hand. But he didn't push the button. "I don't know. In most places, there are all these groups already set up, and they don't let anyone in. And then, if I come into town and make the basketball team, the players don't like me. That's what happened here."

Phil didn't look away. "Some of the guys don't like you. That's true," he said. He hesitated and then added, "But, Aaron, you don't do much to help yourself."

"What do you mean?"

Phil sat down on Aaron's bed. "Never mind. I just—"

"No. Tell me what you mean."

"Well…you give the impression that you think you're too good for them. You *are* better at basketball, but that doesn't mean you can't be friends."

"Who said I don't want to be?"

"You won't talk to anyone, for one thing."

"That's just the way I am. I don't…have a lot to say."

"It's not just that. You don't have anything to do with anyone. And on the court, it's like you think you're the only one out there."

"Oh, come on. The only thing Chris has against me is that I took his position. He doesn't care about being friends."

"Yeah, I guess."

But now Aaron could see that Phil was holding back. "Go ahead. Say what you're thinking. What else does he have against me?"

"Aaron, if you acted like you were really on the team—and not just playing for yourself—he'd be okay about it after a while. Everyone would."

"What are you talking about?"

"Anyone can tell. You're not out there trying to get a win for the team. You want it for yourself."

"Hey, if I win, you guys win."

"Sure, but there's a difference. If you had passed the ball today and Jared had gotten the basket, that wouldn't have been good enough for you. You had to make the basket yourself. And that's what the guys don't like about you."

Aaron told himself that it wasn't true. But he was suddenly very uncomfortable. "I was just..." But Aaron wasn't sure what he wanted to say. Finally, he mumbled, "It's not like you think."

"What isn't?"

Aaron actually had no idea what he meant. He sat down on the floor and leaned against the wall. He wanted to explain to Phil, but he had never really thought it out. "I have to start over every year—sometimes twice in a year. And it seems like I get worse at it every time. I don't know how to talk to people."

"You're so good at basketball, guys will like you if you just hang around with them a little. You don't have to talk all that much."

"It doesn't work that way," Aaron said. "I

give all my time to basketball because that's the one thing I know I'm good at. But as soon as I show what I can do, everybody starts calling me a hot dog. They don't like some new guy being better than they are."

"Yeah. I'm sure guys are jealous of you. But right from the beginning, you acted like you wanted to show us up. That's what made everyone mad."

"I was trying to show I could help the team—that I deserved to play, even if I did get here in the middle of the season."

Phil seemed to think that over, and then he said something that Aaron didn't expect. "That first day, most of the guys thought you were cocky. I was the only one who thought you were just scared."

"Scared? What am I scared of?"

"I don't know exactly. But that's how you seemed to me."

Aaron stared at Phil. He almost denied the whole thing, but he realized that Phil had discovered something about him.

"So how could I get to be friends around here?" he finally asked, feeling embarrassed.

"There's a dance at the school tonight. You can go with me and some of the other guys."

But Aaron felt himself panic. "I don't know how to dance," he said.

"Hey, none of us do—not really. Mostly we just stand around."

Aaron thought that sounded pretty stupid. And frightening.

"So do you want to go?"

"Naw. I don't think so."

"Come on. Give it a shot. What can it hurt?"

"Not tonight. Not after what happened at the game today."

So the boys watched the video. And then Phil left, and Aaron spent the rest of the evening in his room. But the whole time, he wished that he had said that he would go.

chapter eight

At school on Monday, a lot of the kids came up to Aaron and told him what a great player he was. Aaron thanked them, and he concentrated on trying to sound friendly. But he still couldn't think of much to say.

Phil hung around with Aaron quite a bit, especially at lunch. He even took him to the table where most of the basketball players sat. But everything felt awkward. No one mentioned the game, but Aaron was pretty sure they were still upset with him.

The talk was that the next game was a tough one. The Westport Beavers were supposed to be the best team in the league. "They have a guy named Brian Everett who can really play," Chris said. "He's as good as Reeves *thinks* he is."

Chris laughed and so did most of the other guys—sort of nervously.

Aaron thought about telling the guy to shut his mouth. But he said nothing. And Phil was quick to say, "Aaron's better than Everett, if you ask me." But no one brought up the fact that Aaron would start the game on the bench.

Aaron knew these guys were already expecting to lose—and they didn't care that much. That was one thing he could give them—a real desire to win—if they were willing to learn from him. But he knew that wasn't going to happen. Chris had his position back, and everyone was satisfied.

Aaron picked up his tray and left. He knew he had no chance with these guys now—no matter what Phil said.

The week was difficult for Aaron. He practiced hard and looked good, as always. But he worked out with the second team. He played tough defense against the first team, but he was careful not to get too aggressive.

And when the second team went on offense, he passed more than he shot. He tried to prove to the coach that he could find the open man and hit him.

The coach praised him for some of his

passes, but the guy was never satisfied. "The point is not just to pass—but to get the *best* shot," he told Aaron. "If you've got it, take it."

Aaron wanted to say, "Make up your mind, will you?" But he just kept passing. It was his way of letting the coach see the truth. Every time one of the guys on the team missed an easy shot, Aaron wanted to shout, "See! They can't shoot."

The game against the Beavers was a home game for the Timber Wolves. The crowd was bigger than Aaron had ever seen before.

When the first team took off their warmups, Aaron heard a lot of kids yell, "Let Reeves play." But he took his seat as far away from the coach as he could get. And he watched the Timber Wolves get chewed up pretty badly in the early part of the game.

The Beavers had a good-sized team. But Everett was more than half their offense. He had lots of moves. He was tall, but he was also a great jumper, and he could put the ball in the hoop. Aaron could see that he was sure of himself—probably used to doing just what he wanted out there.

Aaron wanted a chance to take him on.

The score was 13–5, and the first quarter was almost over before the coach finally gave

Aaron his chance. He called Aaron down to him, and he said, "That Everett kid is just too quick for Chris. Go in and see what you can do against him."

Aaron pulled off his warmup jacket and raced to the scorer's table. He wished a whistle would blow immediately. He couldn't wait to get out there. And when he finally ran onto the floor, he pointed at Everett, as if to say, "I'm here now. Look out." But he didn't say a word.

The first time Everett got the ball, Aaron faced him, square, ready for any move. Everett gave him a head fake and tried to drive to the left.

But Aaron had been watching his moves. He was looking for the drive to the baseline. He cut Everett off. When the big guy couldn't get to the hoop, he tried to pull up and shoot a fall-away jumper. But Aaron had a hand in his face, and the shot was short.

As the two ran down the court together, Everett smiled at Aaron. "So you think you can stop me, don't you?"

Aaron didn't answer, but he smiled a little. Both of them knew that the contest was on.

But Aaron didn't shoot. He ran the plays, and he passed off. Everett was all over him, and that only made him want to shoot all the more. But he knew what he had to do. The coach had wanted him to "play with the offense," and that's what he was doing.

Everett didn't score the rest of the quarter, but the Timber Wolves didn't gain much ground. No one was shooting very well, and the Beavers played tough defense. All the same, the score was 16–9, and the Beavers weren't running away from them anymore.

Everett had struggled even to get the ball. When he did get a pass, Aaron was quick enough to take away the easy shots he had been getting against Chris.

The Timber Wolves gathered in a huddle during the break between quarters. Coach Newey looked at Aaron. "Hey, good job on Everett," he said. "Keep it up. But what are you doing on offense? I didn't tell you not to shoot."

Aaron shrugged, but he didn't say anything. He had known that the coach would start asking him to shoot, sooner or later, once he saw what his "passing game" produced.

When Aaron walked back on the floor, he knew it was show time. He was going to put some moves on Everett.

The first time he got the ball, he looked around, as though he were going to pass off, and then suddenly he drove past Everett and straight to the hoop. He arched a high shot over the center.

The shot dropped, and the Timber Wolves' fans showed their excitement. The score was 16–11. Aaron thought he could turn things around fast now.

Everett ran alongside Aaron again. "You took me by surprise. But that's the last time. I'm shutting you down."

Aaron smiled at him again, as if to say, "We'll see."

As the Beavers set up their offense, Everett drifted toward the guards and took a pass. He was way outside, and Aaron was staring him in the face. Everett dribbled slowly, crouching, then he broke toward the key, dribbling with his right hand.

Aaron stayed with him, but the center set a solid screen. Aaron fought through—but not quite quickly enough. Everett put up a jump hook that swished the net.

"Now I'm getting serious," Everett told Aaron.

Aaron had to get another basket this time

down the floor. In Everett's face.

Still, he stayed with the play, and the rotation was to the left side. Jared ended up taking a shot from the side of the key. The ball hung on the rim and then rolled off.

Aaron broke to the basket and jumped high for the rebound. He came down with the ball, but Everett was there, between him and the basket.

Aaron faked in the air, but Everett held his ground.

So Aaron took a dribble away from the basket, spun, and put up a fade-away shot over Everett's outstretched arm.

The shot was a little short, and Everett was right there for the rebound. He came down smiling.

Aaron's hand suddenly shot out and knocked the ball from Everett's hands. The ball bounced once and came straight up to Aaron.

Everett's reaction was to go straight for the block. So Aaron took a step and swung a little underhanded shot around Everett. The ball kissed off the glass and went in.

The crowd screamed.

And Everett wasn't smiling.

Aaron knew he had shown the guy up, and

now this little battle was going to get serious.

But Coach Newey stood up and yelled, "Reeves! Don't try to do it by yourself."

What was that supposed to mean? What did the guy want?

Through the rest of the half, Aaron and Everett guarded each other tough, nose-to-nose. But Everett kept shooting, and Aaron had gone back to passing. He didn't know what the coach wanted from him, but he wasn't going to be accused of shooting too much again.

Everett was missing more shots than he was making. The only problem was, the Timber Wolves' players weren't putting the shots down—not as many as they could. The game was getting closer, but Greenwood could never quite pull even.

By halftime the score was 27–25. In the locker room, the Timber Wolves' players seemed excited. "We can get these guys," Jared kept saying.

He even slapped Aaron on the back and said, "Great defense. No one has ever played Everett that tough."

Aaron liked that in a way. Without saying it, Jared was probably thanking Aaron for not shooting so much. But it was all so stupid. Aaron could have had his team up ten points by now.

The coach said, "Okay, we've made up a lot of ground, which means we're doing the right things. Let's just keep it up. Aaron, you're doing a great job on Everett, but I still don't understand what you're doing on offense. Take the good shot when you get it."

Aaron couldn't believe it. No matter what he did, it was wrong. But he nodded and said, "Okay."

At the same moment, he heard Chris whisper, not so softly, "Don't worry, he will."

Something shut down in Aaron. What did it take with these guys?

And so, as the second half started, he worked hard, but he didn't shoot. And the game stayed very tight. Phil was getting open, and he hit a couple of shots. Jared began to score a little, too. But the Timber Wolves still weren't getting a lot of points.

What was keeping the game close was that Everett was getting frustrated. He was still taking most of the shots, but he was forcing them, trying to prove that he could score on Aaron. And he was missing.

The other Beavers' players were a little out of sync, too, as though they were accustomed to riding on Everett's scoring. They didn't know quite what to do when he wasn't hitting.

The whole third quarter was a battle. Aaron and Everett were beginning to bang each other a little more, and each got called for a foul.

Everett wasn't talking now, but he was trying everything to shake Aaron loose. He got a couple of shots to fall, but nothing was easy. His coach had begun to yell to him to pass off.

Aaron kept driving and then dishing off. The problem was, his teammates weren't coming through. Twice he hit Darren with good passes, and the guy threw up wild shots, clear over the rim.

When the third quarter ended, the score was 40–37, with the Beavers still hanging on to the lead. Aaron knew he could take over in this last quarter, and he could win the game.

And get chewed out for it.

He really didn't know what to do.

chapter nine

As the players walked onto the court to start the fourth quarter, Everett walked over to Aaron. "We're going to put you away now, Reeves," he said.

So Everett knew his name now. Aaron liked that. But he didn't say anything. He didn't want to let this guy get to him.

And so the game stayed close in the fourth quarter, with the Beavers staying ahead by two to five points but never breaking away. Everett had finally started to pass off a little more. And maybe he had gotten a little tired, because Aaron was starting to get open more easily. He shot a little more, and he hit his shots. That's what was keeping the Timber Wolves in the game.

But time was running down, and Aaron could feel his hunger to win. He wanted to get a run going—without getting everyone mad at him.

With about two minutes to go, Aaron got open in the corner. It was a long shot, but he had a good look at the basket, and he couldn't resist. He took the shot and banged it home. It was a three-pointer, and suddenly the lead was down to one point.

Everett didn't say anything this time. But Aaron saw the look on his face. He wanted the ball.

And he got it.

He broke off a screen and took a pass right at the foul line. Aaron slipped through the screen and cut Everett off before he could move to the hoop.

Everett went straight up for a jumper, with Aaron all over him. The shot dropped, and the referee called Aaron for the foul.

Everett hit the foul shot and the lead was back to four.

Aaron was mad at himself. But the worst part was, Everett wanted to talk again. He got behind Aaron as he set up on offense. "It's over, Reeves," he said. "You ain't scoring again. I'm the man here."

"That's what you think," Aaron said out loud, and suddenly he didn't care what the coach said. He was going to show this guy, and he was going to win this game somehow—whatever it took.

He cut through the middle of the key and took a pass on the left side. He looked around, as though he was going to pass, and then he broke back to the middle. When Everett took him on, Aaron did his three-sixty spin-dribble move and laid the ball up with his left hand.

And in!

The lead was back to two, and Aaron had made Everett look stupid. He loved it.

Now Everett was going to find out who "the man" was. The coach could chew him out all he wanted—and put him back on the bench next game—but Aaron was going to get this one.

He got on Everett at the other end of the floor, played him so close that the point guard couldn't get the ball to him. "You're finished, Everett," he growled. "You're not going to touch the ball again."

The pass went to the other side, and the other forward put a shot up. Everett sliced to the basket, and so did Aaron, and the two went up together. But Everett outjumped him and came down with the ball. And then he went hard up to the hoop.

Aaron had to foul him to stop the put-back.

Everett had two shots coming. As he shouldered past Aaron, on his way to the foul line, he said, "I guess I got the ball, didn't I?"

Aaron was furious with himself. He was going to get this guy yet.

Everett hit his first foul shot, and the lead was three, 55–52. But he missed the second.

Aaron swept the rebound off the rim, and then he blasted down the court, dribbling. Everett ran with him, but Aaron surprised him by pulling up at the three-point line and taking the shot.

And it was in all the way. The ball snapped into the net, and the score was tied, 55–all.

Aaron made a quick move to the point guard and tried to steal the inbounds pass. He didn't get there quite in time, so he charged hard down the floor, catching up with Everett.

He glanced at the clock. Under a minute to go.

The Beavers' point guard took his time getting into the forecourt, and then he called time out.

Aaron was in his own world. He glanced at the bleachers and saw the kids standing and screaming. But he didn't care about that. He had his own reasons for wanting this game.

Up at the top of the bleachers, Aaron saw his mom. But she wasn't cheering. She looked serious, maybe even worried.

The coach was pounding on his usual theme. "Aaron, be careful right here. You got that shot to fall, but it wasn't the right shot to take."

"Hey, we're tied," Phil said.

But the coach told him to be still and listen. "Don't foul that little guard, and don't foul Everett, but if anyone else gets the ball, go after it. If we pick up a foul on one of the other guys, it's worth the chance they'll miss at least one shot."

Then he talked about what they should do when they got the ball. "If they miss a shot, don't call time out. Crash the boards and then try to get a fast break. Phil, you break quickly and look for the pass. Push the ball hard and go for something off the early offense."

"What if they hit a shot?" Phil asked.

"Then call time out, and we'll set something up."

And so the boys walked back onto the

court. The Beavers passed the ball in, and the point guard dribbled straight down the court to the top of the key. Then he passed to the other guard. They weren't using up time. They were setting up a play.

And it was bound to go to Everett. Aaron covered him tight, staying with him as he broke to the middle. The pass was there, but so was Aaron. He reached out and knocked the ball away. Jared grabbed it, and Phil took off.

Jared tossed the ball long.

Too long.

The ball flew over Phil's outstretched hands and kept on going. It bounced to the other end of the court and out of bounds. The Beavers were going to get the ball back.

Aaron couldn't believe it. He had done what he had to do, and these idiots he had to play with couldn't do their part. His only chance was to get hold of the ball and take care of business himself.

Another time-out. The Beavers were going to set up another play.

Only thirty-six seconds left. Coach Newey said the Beavers would probably try to use the clock up this time and then take a shot with just a few seconds left. Everything was almost the same. Take the foul, but try not to foul Everett or the point guard.

This time, when the action started, Aaron had the feeling that Everett would be the decoy. Someone else was going to take the shot. And sure enough, the point guard let the time run, and then, with about ten seconds left, the offense went into a weave. And the pass was to the other forward, on the left side.

Darren fouled him, going for the steal.

That was good. Aaron knew that the coach was right. The guy wasn't a good foul shooter. Aaron thought he might miss both shots under pressure.

Six seconds were left. Aaron knew he had enough time if he could get hold of the ball.

The forward hit the first shot, however, and that added some pressure.

But he missed the second one.

Aaron leaped high and pulled the rebound down.

And he took off. He dribbled the ball himself, pushing through the maze of running players, going all out. He was going to take it all the way to the hoop.

But Everett was fast, and he dug hard to get ahead of Aaron. Aaron was losing his angle to the basket.

He saw Phil running on the outside, taking a lane.

For an instant Aaron thought of passing to him, but he just couldn't do it.

He suddenly cut off his drive and went up for the jumper. He was off balance, moving fast, but he adjusted in the air, got himself straight, hung on an extra fraction of a second, and then let the shot fly.

It hit the front of the rim, bounced, and then rolled all the way round the iron.

For a moment Aaron thought it was coming out. But just as the buzzer sounded, it dropped through the hoop. The Timber Wolves had won.

Suddenly Phil had hold of Aaron—hugging him, lifting him in the air. And somewhere, over by the basket, Everett was standing with his hands on his hips, looking at the floor.

And then, Aaron got mobbed.

The bleachers emptied, and it seemed that all the students in the middle school were trying to get to him—slap him on the back, yell to him, grab him if they could.

Aaron had some sense that his teammates

were leaving the floor without him, but he couldn't get away. He kept saying, "Thanks. Thanks," as he pushed toward the locker room. But he was a long time making it through the crowd.

When Aaron finally got off the floor and through the locker room doors, he was glad to hear that the players were whooping it up, too.

He walked toward them, still smiling but unsure. Phil told him, "Great game!" And some of the other guys slapped him on the back.

"Nice shot," Darren said. "I never thought it would go down. I don't know how you did it."

Aaron thanked Darren, but he was watching Chris, who had sat down and was already pulling his shoes off. He mumbled something that Aaron didn't hear. But he could tell it wasn't anything friendly.

Suddenly Aaron lost it. He flew at Chris. And he shoved him hard. "What did you say?" he shouted.

Chris caught himself before he fell off the bench, and then he came up quickly, nose-to-nose with Aaron.

"What did you say?" Aaron demanded again.

"I said you had no business taking that shot. Phil had a lane to the hoop, but *you* had to be the hero."

"Phil would have missed it," Aaron shouted into Chris's face, before he thought about what he was saying.

"How do you know that?"

"I passed off to you guys all through the game. But no one can shoot. So I finally took over, and that's why we won."

Chris laughed and shook his head. And then he sat back down on the bench. "Aaron, you're a good player. No one says you aren't. But you're also a jerk."

Aaron couldn't think of one thing to say.

Everyone was around him, looking at him. And he knew they were all agreeing with Chris.

Maybe they were right, too.

chapter ten

Aaron was pushing his way through the locker room doors when the coach stopped him. "Wait a minute, Reeves," he said. And then he asked him to walk into his office.

Aaron didn't want this. He just wanted to get away and have some time to think. But he followed the coach back past all the players and into the little office.

The coach sat down behind his desk. His balding head was covered with sweat, and the neck of his white shirt was wet. "I heard what went on between you and Chris," he said. "I want to know how you feel about it."

Aaron shrugged. He didn't want to talk

about this. He hadn't meant exactly what he had said to Chris—at least not the way it had sounded—but it was pretty hard to take back at this point.

"Did you see Phil when you were running that break, there at the end?"

"Yeah."

"Do you think you should have passed to him?"

Aaron thought for a while. But the whole thing was too complicated. He could never say anything in his defense that the coach would understand. "I guess I should have," he finally said.

"But you thought you were more likely to make the jump shot than he was to make the lay-up?"

"I don't know. Something like that."

"You might be right, too. Or at least you did make it. And who knows, maybe he would have missed. You're certainly a better shooter than he is."

The words seemed to say that Aaron was right, but the tone said something else.

"Isn't that about right?"

"Coach, I know you're supposed to hit the guy with the lane to the basket. I had the defense sucked in on me, and he was open. I saw that. But he didn't have a sure thing. It was not like some simple lay-up. He's not all that fast, for one thing."

"So it's a judgment, isn't it? In one case, it might be better to pass off. In another, taking the jumper is the better-percentage shot. You didn't have a lot of time to make your decision."

Aaron shrugged again. The coach reached over and pulled a hand towel off the back of a chair. He wiped his forehead with it.

"So did you do the right thing?"

"It worked."

"Did you do the right thing, Aaron? Tell me."

"I think so. But I know you don't."

The coach wrapped the towel around his neck. "I wouldn't say that. Maybe it was the right thing in that case. You have a lot of confidence to take a shot like that. But I am worried about what you said to Chris out there."

"I was mad."

"And so you said what you really thought."

Aaron looked down at the floor, away from the coach's eyes.

"And you're right. We've got a better

chance of winning if you do most of the shooting."

The coach let that sit for a time. But Aaron knew he wasn't finished.

"Aaron, I need to tell you a few things. And I want you to think about them."

"Okay."

"One of the marks of a great player is that he makes the guys around him better. And you're not doing that. You passed up a lot of shots early in the game, and then later, you took any shot you could get. Explain that to me."

"You told me to pass, so that's what I was doing."

"Aaron, think about it. I didn't tell you to pass. I told you to get the ball to the open guy if *you* were covered. You weren't trying to make the team work. You were just trying to prove to me that you could pass. And I think you were hoping things would go worse that way—not better."

Aaron was suddenly embarrassed. The coach was right, for the most part. It's just that the whole thing had been a lot more confusing at that time than it seemed now.

"Aaron, when you're on that floor, you're

thinking 'How can I win this game?' not 'How can *we* win this game?' Maybe I'm old-fashioned, but I happen to think one of the great things about sports is creating a team—a bunch of kids who believe in each other and even like each other. I think it's fun to put a game plan together and then to carry it out as a unit, everyone working together."

Aaron had heard plenty about that, but he never had believed it. It all seemed like a lot of pretty talk—something a losing coach told his kids to make them feel better.

But Aaron didn't say that. In fact, he wondered what it would be like to work with some of the guys that way.

"Aaron, you need to make friends with this team. If you won't do that, you'll never be part of it—win or lose."

"I want to be friends," Aaron said weakly.

"You sure don't show it."

Aaron wished he knew how to explain. The coach didn't know what his life was like.

"Here's what I want, Aaron. I want you to start the next game. And I want you to think about winning as a group. That may mean that you take most of the shots, and it may mean that you don't shoot at all. That will depend on the defense, and on the way the game goes. But I want you to be a team member. Either that, or I want you to quit. Think about it, and let me know by Monday what you want to do."

Aaron nodded, and then he got up.

"But I hope you'll play with us. It's a thing of beauty to watch what you can do with a basketball. You have a chance to be a *great* player. You just have to get your head on straight."

Aaron got up. He mumbled, "Thanks," and he meant for the compliments, and even for the talk. But he was still sort of confused. He had a lot to think about.

Outside the office, Phil was waiting. Aaron was really surprised by that.

"Are you okay?" Phil asked.

"Sure," Aaron said, and he wanted to apologize for what he had said earlier, but he wasn't sure how to do that.

As they walked out of the locker room, Phil said, "Look, Aaron, you were right to take that shot. I might have gotten to the hoop, but most likely, I would have gotten fouled. And then I would have had to hit the two foul shots. Under pressure, I don't know if I could have done that."

"I could have missed, too. I almost did. Look what happened last week."

"Aaron, you have twice as much confidence as I do. The guy who believes in himself is the best one to take a shot in a situation like that."

Aaron walked down the hall thinking, and by the time he got outside, he finally knew what he wanted to say. "Phil, I've gotten so I only trust myself. Maybe that's confidence, in a way, but it's not good. It's not what I really want."

"I know what you mean. I have the same problem."

Aaron was taken by surprise. "Really?" he said.

"Yeah. I only trust in you, too. And that's not what I want either." And then he laughed.

But Aaron didn't smile. That was just the point. He did create that feeling in his teammates. Now he wished he could take back what he had said before.

He thought of telling Phil, "You would have made the shot." But he wasn't sure he believed that.

"Hey, we won," Phil said. "Let's just go from there."

Aaron nodded, but then he said, "I need to think about some things."

"Okay. But let your brain rest tonight. There's a party at Robin's house. She asked me to invite you. She said I've *got* to get you there somehow."

Aaron took a long breath. That's the last thing he wanted—a party with a lot of people.

But Phil said, "I think most of the players will be there. It would be a good thing for you to show up."

Aaron thought for quite some time before he finally said, "Yeah. Okay."

And then he hoped for the best.

When Aaron got home, his mom was in her little office. He walked in to say hello.

When she looked up from her desk, she smiled. "Well, you got the job done," she said. Then she studied his face for a time before she said, "What did the coach have to say to you after the game?"

"How do you know he said anything?"

"Because there were some things he needed to say. If he's a good coach, he knew that."

Aaron nodded. "He told me I'm not a team player," he said.

"And what do you think about that?"

"Well…he's right. That's kind of obvious."

"I asked how you *felt* about it."

Aaron smiled just a little. "I can't wait to start passing the ball more," he said.

"Aaron, did you tell him how unhappy you are?"

"No."

"Why not?"

"I'm not unhappy."

"That's not how it looks to me, honey."

Aaron didn't know what to say.

"I talked to your dad last night. I told him we need to start thinking about staying in one place for a few years—so you can have some friends during your high school years."

"What did he say?"

"Well, he was tired. He'd put in another long day, and he's going to be late again tonight. So maybe that had something to do with it. But he said he's sick of the moves, too. He's ready to stay in one place."

"Where?"

"Actually, he said some things might work out for him to stay here. Would you like that?"

"I don't know."

It was a very strange thought. What if he

were going to be around Phil and the rest of the guys all the time now. What would *they* think about it? What about Chris?

"Do you like it here?"

But Aaron didn't have an answer to that question either. He said he'd have to think about it, and then he went to his room. And that's when he realized how frightened he was. Maybe, in some ways, it was harder to stay in one place and deal with things than to leave all the time.

chapter eleven

When Aaron and Phil arrived at Robin's house that night, a lot of kids were already there. Aaron didn't even know who Robin was, but when he saw her, he realized he had seen her at school. In fact, she was in one of his classes. She was pretty, too—tall, with long, dark hair, and big, round eyes.

She had a nice smile, too, and now that he remembered her, he knew that she had been flashing her teeth at him all week.

The first thing she said was, "Aaron, you were fantastic today!"

Robin's family room was full of kids, including about half the guys from the team, and most of them turned to look at him. When he played basketball, he enjoyed the attention—out there where he didn't have to talk to anyone. But here, now, he just wanted to disappear.

What he wondered, more than anything, was what the other ballplayers would think. He knew they would be surprised he was with Phil, after what he had said in the locker room.

But Phil told Robin, loudly enough for everyone to hear, "I just wish Aaron had moved here before the season started. We could have won the championship."

Most everyone seemed to agree. Aaron heard compliments coming from all over the room, but he avoided looking directly at anyone. As his eyes passed around the room, however, he spotted Chris, who was talking to Darren and Jared. They were about the only ones not looking at him.

Phil talked to Robin for a minute or two, and then she asked Aaron a few questions about himself. Aaron gave his usual quick answers, and she was soon left with nothing to say. Aaron didn't want that. He even tried to think of something to tell her, just to ease the awkwardness, but he couldn't think of anything, and Phil took over again.

It all seemed so easy for Phil.

After a few minutes, Robin excused herself when some more kids arrived. Aaron was looking toward the couch. He wanted to find a seat and just slip out of sight. He was also a little nervous that dancing might start at some point.

Aaron took a step toward the couch, but Phil grabbed his arm. "Come here," he said, and then he walked straight to the little group of basketball players. Aaron followed, but he dreaded this.

"So how are you guys doing?" Phil said.

The boys all said something, sort of acknowledging Phil, but they didn't look at Aaron.

"At least *you* shouldn't be tired, Chris," Phil said. "You got plenty of bench time today."

It was the last thing in the world Aaron would have brought up. And for a moment, he thought it was a big mistake. But Chris smiled. "Don't get smart, Phil," he said. "I'm going to switch to point guard and beat you out."

"Naw, it wouldn't work. You're good at dribbling spit down your chin—but you can't dribble a basketball."

And that started the usual insults—all of the stuff that guys usually said to each other.

Aaron hated all that, and he stayed out of it. But there he was, like an extra wheel, still standing back a little, wishing he had never come.

And then Phil turned to him and said, "Aaron, do you like the offense that Coach Newey uses?"

This was such an obvious attempt to bring Aaron into the conversation that it embarrassed everyone. Aaron struggled for a moment and then said simply, "It's okay."

But that's when Chris said, "How would you know? You've never tried to use it."

"Come on, Chris," Darren said. "Don't start that."

And then everyone stood in a circle, self-conscious, with no one saying anything.

Aaron took a deep breath, and then he said, "I think we use the high post too much. It pulls Jared too far away from the basket. He's better at powering to the hoop than he is at shooting jumpers."

"Yeah, I've noticed that, too," Darren said. But he had some questions, and soon everyone but Chris was talking back and forth. It quickly became clear that Aaron not only played the game well, but he had thought a lot about it.

And Aaron could feel their respect for what he knew.

But then Jared surprised Aaron. "How did you get to be so good?" he asked.

"I started playing really young," Aaron said. "We were moving all the time, and I didn't have many friends. So I just started shooting hoops by myself all the time. That's what I do now—more than anything."

"Well, it's paid off," Jared said. He was leaning against the wall, with his hands tucked into his jeans pockets.

"Yeah, in a way. But it's not good—you know—to make so much out of one thing."

Darren said, "Why not? That's why you're so good at it."

Aaron wasn't sure he could do this. He had been thinking all afternoon, since the game, and he thought he understood some things about himself. But he wasn't sure he could put them into words. "Well...most of you guys like basketball, but you do other things, too. But for me, basketball is everything. And that's not good. I think it's why I...get messed up sometimes."

Aaron was looking at Chris, and in some way, he meant the words as an apology.

Chris seemed to sense that. He was watching Aaron, but he still didn't say anything.

"When I get out on the court," Aaron said, "I kind of lose control. It's like I *have* to win. And I don't even know why I feel like that."

The boys nodded, as if to say, "Yeah, we know." But something had changed in their faces, as though they were seeing something new in Aaron.

"I should have passed off to Phil today. It's not his fault that I was afraid he'd miss. It's mine." About ten very awkward seconds went by, with no one talking, and then Aaron said, "So anyway...I'm sorry about that."

"Well...you made the shot," Chris said. "I would have missed it."

"I still should have passed off."

And that seemed to signify a truce between the two.

The whole conversation changed from that point. First Jared asked Aaron about some of the teams he had played on, and then they talked about the NBA. But before long they were talking about the middle school, and then Phil said, "Aaron, I think every girl in the school is after you. You're the hottest thing that ever hit this town."

Aaron had felt some of that around the school, and so he didn't deny it. But he told the truth. "I hate talking to girls," he said. "I never know what to say."

"Phil will give you some lessons," Chris said. "He thinks he knows all about it."

"Hey, I do," Phil said. "The whole thing is, you have to be really, really sincere with girls. That's what they like. And it's not that hard to fake."

All the boys laughed, and then Darren said, "Hey, Aaron, I think you're going to get a chance to try it. Here comes Robin."

Music had just begun to play. And now it hit him that he might have to dance. He was suddenly petrified. So he told Robin the truth when she asked. "I don't even know how to dance."

She grabbed him by the arm and dragged him into the middle of the room. "I'll show you," she said. "Any guy who can play basketball the way you do can learn to dance."

Ten minutes later he was dancing. And even sort of liking it. Or at least liking Robin.

On Monday, Aaron told his coach he wanted to play. And that week at practice,

Aaron tried to think differently. He tried to picture the offense as a unit, with the goal being to get one of the five guys in position to take the best possible shot. If he was that guy, fine. If not, he could make the right pass at the right time. That was sort of fun.

The next game was with the Seaside Sharks. So on Friday, the team took the bus to a pretty little town on the ocean. The gym was small, but it was packed, and the fans were almost all from Seaside.

Aaron started the game. As he walked onto the court, he was more nervous than usual. He felt that old urge of his to put on a show for these kids, beat them in their own gym and quiet them down. But he told himself not to think that way. It wasn't his show. The coach said that great players brought the best out of their teammates. That's what he wanted to do today.

All week he had enjoyed the guys, felt as though he finally had some friends. He didn't want to blow that now.

The Timber Wolves got the opening tip, and Phil pushed the ball up the court. Then he passed off to Aaron. Aaron accelerated past his defender so suddenly that he was wide open to the hoop. He took the ball in and laid it up for a quick two.

As the teams ran back to the other end of the court, the Shark center took a pass, faked to a cutting guard, and then tried to roll to the hoop. But Jared held his ground, and the center had to put up an off-balance shot that was off line.

Darren grabbed the rebound and passed off to Phil. He tried to get the break going, but the Sharks dropped back too quickly. He slowed down and dribbled the ball into the forecourt, and the Timber Wolves set up for the half-court offense.

Phil passed to Shawn. Jared moved to his left and set a screen. Aaron scraped off him, open and free. Shawn hit him with a pass, and Aaron went straight up with the jumper. He banged the shot home, and the Timber Wolves were up by four.

And that's how things went for a while. Aaron didn't take all the shots, but he was getting open on almost every play. The guy guarding him just wasn't up to the job. Phil and the others kept feeding him, and Aaron kept popping the net.

He only missed one shot in the first quarter,

and when it was over, the Timber Wolves were up, 17–10. Aaron came off the floor apologizing for shooting so much.

But the coach told him, "Hey, as long as they let you get open, take the shot. You're our best weapon. But don't expect to be that open this next quarter. Their coach has got to make some changes."

chapter twelve

When the second quarter started, Aaron soon found out that he had a new defender. This guy was a little shorter, but he was much quicker than the big guy who had guarded him in the first quarter.

More than that, the first time Aaron got the ball, a second defender moved in on him. That was the challenge Aaron had been waiting for.

He pivoted with the ball, took a look around, and then snapped the ball to Darren, who was open in the corner. Darren took the shot.

And missed everything.

The Sharks' fans really got on him, too. A lot of them started screaming, "Air ball!"

Aaron yelled to him as they ran back down the court, "That's okay, Darren. Don't worry about it."

But Aaron worried a little himself. Darren seemed to shoot well in practice, but he had trouble when the pressure was on. The Sharks were probably going to leave him open and take their chances that he wouldn't beat them the way Aaron would.

The old feeling was suddenly there. Aaron didn't want to lose the lead he had built up.

The Sharks' center missed a shot, and Aaron grabbed the rebound. The Timber Wolves went on the offense again.

But once they set up their offense, Aaron could see that Darren was alone again. The Sharks were daring the Timber Wolves to go to him.

Phil did pass to him, but Darren didn't want to shoot. He tried to pass to Jared, in the middle, and the Sharks stole the ball.

They broke quickly and drove the ball up the floor. Aaron got in the middle of the break, and so did Phil, but it was three-on-two. The guard made the right pass and one of the forwards took the ball all the way in for the score.

The score was 17–12 now, but Aaron could feel that the Sharks were coming alive. They were really getting active on defense. His own defender was staying right on top of him.

On offense, Phil tried to take the rotation to the right, and Aaron tried to slip off the screen the way he had early in the game. But the defenders switched off perfectly, and a second defender broke to Aaron.

He went up for the shot anyway—or seemed to. But he passed instead. He tried to hit Jared near the basket. But Jared had been expecting the shot instead of the pass. He reacted too slowly and the ball slipped through his hands and out of bounds.

If only these guys could play ball!

Aaron talked to himself—told himself not to think that way. But he was frantic to get the ball back before the Timber Wolves blew their lead.

When the Sharks' guard tried to get the ball to Aaron's man, Aaron tried to cut in and steal the ball. He got the ball, all right, but he also hit his man hard with his body, and the ref called the foul.

It wasn't a shooting foul, but when the Sharks threw the ball in, the shooting guard fired from outside and hit a three-pointer.

Aaron looked at the scoreboard. The lead was only two, 17–15, and he could feel all his work slipping away. Maybe passing off to these guys meant losing on purpose.

And so he worked to get free this time, and when he got the ball in his hands, he took his shot. And it should have been in. It seemed to go down, but it popped back out.

Nothing wrong with that. That happened sometimes. The important thing was, he had gotten off a decent shot, even if it was in the middle of a crowd.

He got back on defense and really hustled. And this time he sagged away from his man and darted into the middle. He knocked a pass away and Jared grabbed it.

He took off down the floor and got the lead pass from Jared.

Then he drove all the way, even though a defender was all over him. He went hard to the hoop and got his basket. Plus a foul.

Now he was rolling. The lead was back to four, and soon it would be five.

But the coach was calling from the sidelines that he wanted a time-out. As Aaron walked off the court, he knew what he was going to hear.

The coach didn't give any speeches, however. He only said, "Aaron, think it over.

Think what you want to do."

And then he talked to all the players. "Darren," he said, "they're going to give you that shot from the corner. And you can hit it. You do all the time in practice. Just relax."

Darren nodded, but he took a deep breath, as though he weren't so sure.

"And Jared, when you set a pick and the defense doubles Aaron, you roll to the hoop and look for the pass. They can't cover everyone if they double on Aaron. You guys are going to have some fun today."

Aaron, meanwhile, was talking to himself. He knew Darren had to build his confidence. He wasn't used to shooting very much. And Jared had to get used to the pick and roll, since he hadn't gotten the ball back from Aaron very often in the past.

It could work. It really could. Aaron just had to give it time.

But the rest of the half was a struggle. Darren missed two more shots from the corner. And Jared got a chance for an easy lay-up and banged the ball too hard off the glass.

Jared did get one shot to go down, and Phil hit a jumper, but Aaron was getting nothing, and the team was all out of sync.

By halftime the score was 27–23. The Sharks had taken over the lead.

Aaron expected to hear some chewing out at halftime, but the coach joked with the team. "Hey, we've got 'em where we want 'em now," he said. "They think Darren can't shoot. But he's going to drive them crazy in the second half."

Darren looked anything but pleased with that idea. He sat with his head down, and Aaron could sense the pressure he was feeling.

As the guys walked back out to warm up for the second half, Aaron walked alongside Darren. "You were kind of pushing the ball in the first half," Aaron said. "You don't usually do that. Take a few warmup shots and snap your wrist, the way you do in practice. The shot will go down."

Aaron stood next to him as they shot around before the game started again. "That's it," he kept saying when Darren's motion was right—even if he missed the shot.

And he did start to hit some. Aaron didn't know what to expect when the game got going, but he did like trying to give Darren some help.

And so, the first time Aaron got the ball in

the second half, he snapped the ball over to Darren in the corner.

And Darren took the shot.

It looked like it was going down, but it was a little long, and it bounced off the rim.

Still, the motion had been right, and Aaron shouted, "Good shot, Darren. You'll get the next one."

But the Sharks got the ball inside and the center scored on a good move to the hoop. The lead was up to six, and Aaron hoped the Sharks didn't get away from them now.

When the Timber Wolves set up on offense, no defender even bothered with Darren. Aaron saw Phil look at Darren and then look away.

Aaron called out, "Hit Darren. He's open!"

Phil passed into the corner, and this time Darren looked as if he meant it. He squared up, jumped straight, and he snapped his wrist just right.

The shot hit the net, and Aaron went straight in the air. "That's it, Darren. You're the man!" he yelled.

Darren was yelling, "All right, let's play some defense now." And Aaron could hear his confidence.

The Timber Wolves' defense picked up immediately. When the pass came to the center, Jared was all over the guy. He forced a shot that fell short of the rim, and Darren was there for the rebound.

The Timber Wolves came hard, as the defense got back. But there was Darren, open in the corner again. Phil delivered the quick pass, Darren hit the shot again, and the lead was down to two.

At the other end of the floor, the shooting guard ended up taking a long shot, and he missed. Aaron cleared the board, and the Timber Wolves went back on offense.

The Sharks' coach was up yelling to his team to cover "number twenty-one in the corner."

So Phil took the play the other way. Aaron came off the screen and picked up an extra defender. But Jared rolled to the hoop and looked back. Aaron shot the ball to him, and Jared got the easy lay-up.

The game was tied, and the Sharks' coach was yelling for a time-out. But Aaron knew. So did all the Timber Wolves. They were going to win this game.

The Sharks had to cover Darren now, and they had to watch the pick and roll. And once the defense on Aaron loosened a little, he took his shots when he got them.

In the fourth quarter, after Aaron had sat down for a while and Chris and some of the other subs had gotten some playing time, he came back into the game. The lead had dropped a little, but the Timber Wolves were still safely ahead, 48–37.

When Aaron came down with a long rebound near the foul line, he spun and took off for his own basket. A defender came with him, and both ran hard to the hoop.

Aaron loved this. He loved to take the guy all the way, use one of his tricky lay-ups, and pick up the foul at the same time. But then he spotted Phil, running to his right.

Aaron kept the ball, kept the defender close, and then, just as it seemed he would go up for the shot, dropped the ball off to Phil. Phil was alone for the easy lay-up.

Aaron high-fived Phil, and the two ran back up the court together.

When the game was over and the Timber Wolves had the win, that one play was the one that stuck in Aaron's mind. And the coach seemed to know that. "You had some fun out there today, didn't you?" he asked Aaron.

"Yeah. It felt good," Aaron said. But he was too embarrassed to say much more than that.

And he felt the same way as each of the players, even Chris, took turns telling him what a good game he had played. He liked telling the guys that they had played well, too. And most of all, he liked meaning it.

On the bus, Phil sat by Aaron. The boys talked about how well the team was playing now. "Man, I'd give anything to have you be here the next few years—all the way through high school. We could really be good."

"Actually," Aaron said, "my dad's been talking about staying here. I'm not sure, but I might be back next year."

Phil jumped right out of his seat. "Hey, guys!" he shouted. "Guess what? Aaron might be staying in Greenwood."

"All right!" someone shouted, and then everyone began to cheer.

Aaron had never felt so happy in his whole life.